A Bride for Chance

Book Four
Brides of Broken Arrow

Cheryl Wright

A BRIDE FOR CHANCE
Book Four
Brides of Broken Arrow

Copyright ©2022 by Cheryl Wright

Cover Artist: Black Widow Books

Editing: Amber Downey

Dedication

To Margaret Tanner, my very dear friend and fellow author, for her enduring encouragement and friendship.

To Alan, my husband of over forty-six years, who has been a relentless supporter of my writing and dreams for many years.

To Virginia McKevitt, cover artist and friend, who always creates the most amazing covers for my books.

To You, my wonderful readers, who encourage me to continue writing these stories. It is such a joy knowing so many of you enjoy reading my stories as much as I love writing them for you.

Table of Contents

Chapter One

Broken Arrow Ranch, Halliwell, Montana – 1880's

Chance Devlin used his best handwriting, the way he was taught at school.

Dear Teddy,

"Darn it," he said as he screwed up the page and threw it in the wastebasket. "That is far too informal." It wasn't as though he really knew the man. Teddy, Theodore Black, was the Adams brothers' lawyer. He wasn't a friend of Chance, and barely knew him. Just because Jacob had given him permission, and even encouraged him to write to the man, didn't mean niceties should go out the window.

Dear Mr. Black,

I work for Jacob Adams, and he told me to write to you.

Another piece of paper screwed up and thrown in the wastebasket. He really needed to think about this some more. Asking for a proxy bride was not something he really wanted to do, but he wasn't getting any younger, and already over forty, Chance wanted children. That was not going to happen unless he married.

He might have already left it too late.

Chance wasn't even sure why he was doing this. A proxy bride – was that really what he wanted? Sure, it had worked for Noah, Seth, and Jacob, but that didn't mean it would work for him. Chance thought the odds were pretty grim. And just because it worked for those three, didn't mean it would be right for him. Three out of four were pretty good odds, and it would be just his luck that it wasn't the right thing for him to do.

Well, he had to be up with the sun, so he would sleep on it. After all, he didn't have to write that letter tonight. Even if time was slipping away.

He threw another log on the fire, blew out the lantern, and slipped into the cold and empty bed that faced him each and every night.

Chance sat quietly contemplating supper. Most nights it was beans and bacon, but sometimes he made bacon and eggs, or even scrambled eggs with sausages on the side. Either way, he was tired of eating the same boring and simple meals. The loneliness was becoming too much as well.

He had watched his boss, Jacob Adams, go from a lonely man to a happily married man after accepting a proxy bride. Convinced that may not be the right path for him, Chance decided to ponder the problem a little longer.

He pushed a few small logs into the wood stove and poked at them, then filled the kettle. A hot cup of coffee was always appreciated. At least coffee helped to fill in a little of his time, but it didn't stop the absolute loneliness he often felt after a full day of working on the ranch.

Each of the ranch hands at Broken Arrow had their own house. None were large, but they were big enough to accommodate a ranch hand, and even a wife and small family. He'd been on this ranch for well over a decade, and still hadn't managed to fill the rooms, let alone his heart.

He reached for a clean mug, then paused as he heard a knock on the door. He rarely had visitors and wondered who it could be.

Chance headed toward the door as the caller knocked again. He quickly opened the door and found Laura Massey standing there, holding something wrapped in a kitchen towel. She leaned her head back a touch and glanced up at him.

"Hello Chance," she said in that shy way she always seemed to have around him. As she smiled, his heart thudded.

"Evening, Laura." She had arrived on the ranch not long after Chance. Only she'd been employed for a totally different reason – to become nanny to the three boys who had recently lost their mother. He glanced into her face, remembering the beauty she was back then, and still was now. Her responsibilities then were far more than any teenage girl should be burdened with, but it worked both ways, and she was pulled out of a difficult situation too. "What brings you here?" He was never one to mince words, but now felt his words sounded abrupt.

She frowned momentarily, then smiled. "I thought you might like this." She pushed what was in her hands toward him. "Careful, it's still hot," she said, then turned to leave.

He lifted the kitchen towel briefly, and the aroma of freshly made stew permeated his senses. "Thank you," he said, genuinely grateful. It wasn't the first time she'd brought supper for him, and he'd appreciated it then as well. "There's plenty here. Did you want to stay and share a meal with me?" The moment the words were out, he realized he might sound pushy. Besides, Laura would be risking her reputation dining alone with him.

"I…" Her hesitancy told him all he needed to know. "The truth is, I've already eaten," she said firmly. "Maybe some other time. There should be enough there for at least two meals."

"Appreciate it," he said. This time she turned and continued on up the hill toward the big house and didn't turn back.

He watched as she strolled meaningfully back to where she came from, her skirt swaying from side to side. His heart fluttered as he studied every move she made. It cemented his belief he needed a wife.

Chance waited until he could no longer see Laura, then went inside, eager to eat the stew she'd brought him. He cut off two thick slices of bread, then placed one serving of the rich smelling food into a bowl. There was plenty there for seconds should he want it, or a meal for another night. He would see how that played out.

After buttering the bread, he said a silent grace, then tucked in. He heard himself groan out loud at the delicacy that tantalized his taste buds. What he wouldn't give to have the luxury of Laura's meals each and every night. Unfortunately, she was not his to have. She lived in Jacob's house as his housekeeper, and also helped look after Clarissa and Jacob's baby boy, Barnabas.

He'd seen Laura with children – they delighted her, and she pleased them. As far as he could tell, she was born to be a mother, but the way things were going, that would never happen. Such a pity.

Chance shook his head and rolled his shoulders. He needed to get this delicious meal in his belly before it went cold. He probably should have been more appreciative when Laura was here, but he never was one much for talking. But then again, he didn't really have anyone to talk to, except maybe the animals when he was out working the ranch.

He sat back when he'd finished eating. It was the most appetizing meal he'd had for ages. A man could certainly get used to that.

It got him to thinking.

Laura stood at the kitchen counter making pastry for the pies she would bake. Two family sized apple pies, and a smaller one – for Chance. He seemed so lonely, and he was losing weight. She'd noticed it a lot lately and was certain he wasn't eating well. Not that she blamed him; she couldn't imagine cooking only for herself. She was certain she would take shortcuts too. Perhaps not eating beans every night – it would never come to that.

She suddenly gasped. *Was he eating out of a tin?* She'd heard a lot of bachelor cowboys did that, and it didn't sit well with her. Jacob wanted his ranch hands to be afforded their privacy, which was the reason their meals weren't provided. But what if they were all eating canned beans for every meal?

She shook herself mentally. It wasn't her problem, and it really wasn't Jacob's either. He was a good boss, providing every ranch hand with a family sized cabin. Not many ranch owners did that. Well, all the Adams men did it – they followed their father's lead. He might be gone, but his example had not been lost on any of his sons. They were all good and fair men, and looked out for their workers, herself included. She didn't think that because she'd brought them up after their mother died so young, it was because they were decent law-abiding and God-fearing men. She was beyond proud of what each one of them had become.

They were good fathers and husbands, as well as being the best at what they did. The *Broken Arrow Ranch* was proof of that. Their father would be beyond proud of them, Laura was certain.

The thought of the men not eating well sat on her mind as she finished off the pies. Should she ask Jacob if she could start providing meals for the men? Or was that asking too much? Then a thought struck her – if she did that, then left the ranch, they would be right back where they started.

But she would never leave the ranch. *Would she?* Laura had arrived here when she was a naive teenager, and had been here ever since. *Would she even survive outside the ranch?* It was not a subject she'd pondered before, but perhaps it was time to give it real thought. What would happen to her if Clarissa suddenly decided she no longer needed help around the house or with the baby?

She shook the thought aside. Clarissa had grown up with maids and other servants. Laura wasn't sure she was even capable of running a house alone. She wasn't being malicious, it was the fact of the matter. Growing up with a personal maid to get her up in the morning, and even to bathe and dress her, coming to *Broken Arrow Ranch* had been an eyeopener for the young mother. Her life had changed dramatically since marrying Jacob by proxy.

Laura shook herself mentally. She had to stop all these ridiculous thoughts. She had plenty to do today, and her runaway thoughts were slowing her down. She had a roast in the oven, but the moment it was ready, the pies would take its place. And she had yet to bake the bread. She glanced across to see it had risen beautifully. There was even an extra loaf there for Chance.

Chapter Two

"This is becoming a habit," Chance said as he gratefully accepted the apple pie and freshly baked loaf of bread from Laura.

Her smile faded. "I…" He'd offended her, which was the last thing on his mind.

"I'm sorry. That sounded ungrateful, and it wasn't meant to." Did she take baked goods to Floyd and Karl, the other two ranch hands? He was almost certain the answer was no. Still, his cabin was the closest to the main house, so perhaps it was just the luck of the draw. "I really appreciate you making these for me and bringing them down here." And he did, he really did. It did make him wonder if Jacob knew, and what he thought about it. Being the decent man he was, Jacob probably didn't mind in the least.

But he could be wrong. The last thing he wanted was for Laura to get into trouble on his account.

"I hope you enjoy them," she said, then turned and began to walk away.

"I know I will." He looked to the sky. It was already getting dark, and although they might be on private property and out of town, you never knew who might be lurking about. "Let me walk you back home."

She turned to face him then, a frown on her face. "It's not far, and I've done it before."

"I'd rather know you were safe. Let me put these inside, and I'll be right back." It didn't take long, and he was by her side. She stood firmly, not moving, even when he began to walk toward the main house. "Is there a problem?" he asked, genuinely perplexed.

"A gentleman lets a lady hook her arm through his," she said quietly, and without malice.

Well, he was a cowboy, not a gentleman, and it had been years since he'd stepped out with a lady so had no idea what was expected of him. "My apologies," he said, then offered his arm. She giggled then, and a thrill ran down his spine. She was joking with him, and it spread warmth through him. He couldn't recall a time where he'd seen her joke before, and it made him feel special.

She suddenly stood in front of him, a huge grin on her face. "I'm not a lady, in case you didn't know," she said, still grinning.

"And I sure ain't no gentleman." He laughed then, joining in the joke. This was a side of Laura Massey he'd never seen before, but he liked it. He was enjoying the fact she'd let her guard down with him.

"Well, here we are," she said when they arrived a short time later. "Thank you for escorting me home. I appreciate it."

"And I appreciate that you are feeding me good food." She smiled then and opened the door. He had the sudden urge to kiss her, but knew she would slap his face if he did.

"Goodnight," she said, and slipped inside without another word.

"Goodnight," Chance said to the empty doorway, wishing she was still there with him.

"I sure do appreciate you inviting me over for Sunday lunch," Chance told Jacob, as he sat down at the table. He still wore his Sunday best as that seemed appropriate. Moments later Floyd and Karl arrived, which didn't surprise him in the least.

When there was a family picnic, Jacob's workers were always invited, and if there was a party going on, they were invited to that too. The truth was, Jacob treated his workers as though they were family.

"Don't thank me," Jacob responded. "It was all Laura's idea." He didn't seem unhappy about it in the least, which was a huge relief. The last thing Chance wanted was to think that Jacob had been pressured into it. But then again, Laura wasn't like that.

She was a sweet lady with cooking skills, the likes of which he'd never experienced before. She was only a few years younger than Chance but had aged well. To him, she didn't look much older than when she'd arrived far too many years ago, unlike himself. His eyes followed her as she moved around the room.

"Did you hear what I said, Chance?" Floyd's voice seemed to bellow, bringing him out of his daydream.

"Yes, sure, I agree," he said, having absolutely no idea what he was agreeing too.

Laughter spread around the room, and he wanted to crawl under the table. "Right, so tomorrow we'll fill your shoes with cow pats and watch you put them on."

"What?" Chance felt a blanket of heat crawl up his face, making him want to sink down inside the floor. He shook his head then, realizing Floyd was making fun of him. *What had grabbed his attention anyway?* Oh, right, it was Laura.

It begged the question; when did he start to notice the petite woman who's cooking gripped at his taste buds? It was far too many years ago, and he knew it. He'd forced himself to stop longing for her way back when, because she was occupied with bringing up three very young and very innocent boys. She didn't have time for the likes of him.

Not that he'd asked. He knew she couldn't have her attention taken away from her precious charges. But those boys were adults now, and it got him to thinking that perhaps she had the time now.

Or perhaps not. She was now nanny for young Barnabas – Jacob and Clarissa's baby. Plus she had the household to run, as she'd been doing for some years now.

It seemed to Chance there would never be a good time for him to even think about courting Laura. No matter when he thought about it, she was busy.

She reached across the table and placed a platter with a large piece of roasted beef, and roasted vegetables around it. Then she returned to the kitchen and brought out a roasted chicken and placed that next to the beef. As she straightened,

Laura sighed, then glanced about, possibly deciding if everything that needed doing had been done. Then she reached over and began to pull out the chair next to him, the only vacant chair at the table.

At almost the same moment, Chance stood and hauled out the chair, their fingers brushing slightly. A shiver ran down his spine. "Allow me, Laura." Her cheeks turned a pretty shade of pink, and she said not a word, nodding his way instead. When he was assured she was comfortably seated, Chance took his place at the table once again.

When everyone was settled, Jacob spoke. "Please join hands while we say grace." He glanced up and when he was happy everyone had complied, he spoke again. "Bless this food, Lord, and for the friends who have joined us today. Amen."

Chance glanced down at Laura's hand that was intertwined with his and wondered if she'd felt the same kind of warmth he felt. He glanced at her, and she smiled. *Did that mean anything?* He really wasn't certain.

"Dig in, everyone. We don't want the food to go cold."

"It looks delicious," Chance said, more to Laura than anyone.

Floyd added to the conversation. "It certainly does. Thank you, Laura. You must have spent most of the day in the kitchen." *Was Floyd trying to win points with Laura?* It wasn't something he'd even thought about before, but Chance would need to heed the warning. The other cowboy was probably as interested in the charming spinster as Chance was.

"Thank you both," she said, glancing from one to the other. "Most of it cooked itself while we were all at church."

Chance lifted one of the platters, the one with the beef and roasted vegetables, and held it in place for Laura to serve herself. She took hardly enough to feed a sparrow, and he stared down at her plate. "Surely that's not enough." It was a statement rather than a question. She simply smiled at him and looked away.

He placed the platter back into the center of the table, feeling confused. How could she survive on such a small amount of food?

"Would you pass the chicken please, Chance?" She smiled at him now, and his heart thudded. She helped herself to a drumstick, and then a serving of beans when he passed them over. Lastly she added gravy.

When he was certain Laura had all she wanted, he filled his own plate. She was a magnificent cook. He'd always known it but couldn't recall having a roast meal here before. If it wasn't apple pie, she would bring him left over stew, or thick vegetable soup. He didn't care what it was she brought to him, it was all delicious. If a man wasn't careful, he could find himself putting on more weight than was good for him.

Friendly banter went around the table, with talk of young Barnabas, as well as some ranch talk. Jacob didn't get involved in ranch business much, but liked to hear what was going on. His interest was in the bookkeeping side of the ranch. He wasn't an outdoors person at all. Even as a young boy, Chance couldn't recall him spending much time with the animals. He seemed to have a special dislike for the horses. Then he recalled the incident that turned him off them. It was Jacob's fault, not the horse's. But he was too young to understand. It was probably far too late now to remedy that. Such a pity.

Chance loved the outdoors. He reveled in looking after the animals, and was constantly amazed he was paid for doing what he loved most. He had spent all of his adult years at *Broken Arrow Ranch*, and it was home to him. He didn't even want to ponder not being there. He'd learned everything he knew from the foreman of the time. Old Charlie had since passed on, but Chance would never forget him.

Laura began to clear the table, and Chance jumped up to help her. "It's fine, Chance," she said quietly. "You sit down and enjoy the company." He felt conflicted then. He wanted to help – Laura had spent a lot of time preparing the meal, and he wanted to show her how much he appreciated it. He stood where he was, not sure how to proceed. Her hand landed on his shoulder, and she gently guided him back to his chair.

He complied, not wanting to make a scene, and she smiled at him, then headed toward the kitchen with the soiled plates. It wasn't long before she was back, this time with desserts, all laid out on a rolling trolley.

There were a variety of desserts, including apple pie, tapioca pudding, and apple shortcake. Laura placed them all on the table, along with a large bowl of clotted cream. The ranch was mostly self-sufficient and knowing most of the ingredients came from the *Broken Arrow Ranch* made them even more enticing.

He stared up at the woman who had made all this happen. He couldn't believe his luck in knowing her, and being the recipient of her wonderful baking. It was then an idea began to form in his mind.

"It was a magnificent meal. Thank you, Laura," he said when the table was cleared away. He had offered to help with the dishes, but she would have none of it, and was promptly herded into the sitting room, along with the other men. Clarissa helped clear the table, and then with the dishes. Soon afterward, the women joined them in the sitting room.

"We should do this again," Jacob said. "Thank you Laura for the suggestion."

"Only next time, I'll help. No protests," Clarissa said firmly. "It's an awful lot of work for one person." Clarissa had mellowed a lot since she'd arrived and was nothing like the entitled brat who arrived over a year ago.

Laura sat on the edge of Chance's chair, and he wasn't sure if he should read anything into that. After all, both Floyd and Karl were also in the room and as accessible as Chance was. She stared down into his face and smiled. His heart thudded at the implication but knew he should take nothing for granted. He glanced up and searched her face. "Would you like to go for a walk?" His voice was low – if she said no, he didn't want the entire room to know about it. After all, it would be like a slap in the face.

But she didn't refuse. She smiled, then reached for his hand. "I'd love that." She stood then, and Chance followed suit. "I just need to grab my shawl and bonnet." She was gone only a short time before returning.

They left the sitting room together without a word. Chance heard low mutterings and wondered if the discussion was about the two of them. "It doesn't matter," Laura told him gently, then led him outside.

The moment the door closed behind them, Laura let out a breath. "I love the fresh air. It's most…invigorating," she said. Chance studied her. She looked far more relaxed now that it was only the two of them. He felt the same. He was never one for craving company and was happy enough with his own company most of the time. But more lately he'd felt loneliness creeping in. He wasn't sure what had triggered it, except it did seem to coincide with Laura's visits to his cottage.

Was that the reason he'd decided to get a proxy bride? He hadn't attempted to write away for a proxy bride again. For some reason, he felt stuck, as though it wasn't really in his heart. He wasn't sure of the reason for that.

Remembering their last walk, Chance offered his arm, and Laura hooked hers through it. "It's a beautiful day," she said, glancing up at the blue sky. "Where should we go?"

"We could wander down to the stream if you'd like." He nearly said, I'll go anywhere provided you go too, but stopped himself in time. *Was that what was really in his heart? Was Laura the woman who was meant for him?* They'd wasted so much time, more than a decade, so he'd best make up his mind.

He either pursued Laura with a view to marriage, or he sent away for a proxy bride. Once he wrote that letter, there was no turning back.

Chance knew in his heart the route he needed to take, but now he needed to make it happen.

Chapter Three

"I love it down here." She had always loved it. From the day she'd arrived, Laura had loved the peacefulness of the stream, and often brought the boys here. All four of them would simply sit on a blanket and take in the quiet. Sometimes they would have a picnic, and often the boys would fall asleep after using up all their energy running around.

There were plenty of family picnics here too, both before and after the boys had married. She inwardly chuckled. Those *boys* were grown men with children of their own. Laura wasn't sure she'd ever stop thinking of them as *her boys*. She was the closest thing they had to a mother, and they were the closest thing she had to children. At her age, it was unlikely she'd ever have children on her own, which was sad, but she'd resigned herself to the fact.

"I can see why." Chance glanced down at her, and his smile lifted her spirits. No matter if she never married, and it seemed highly likely, she would always have her *Broken Arrow* family. The thought warmed her. "Have you ever thought about getting married?" Chance looked shocked at the question he'd just asked and was now frowning. "Sorry, none of my business."

She laughed then. "I think about it a lot, but at my age, no one would be interested. I left it far too late."

"You and me both." He pushed his cowboy hat back and scratched his head then, as though he didn't know where the words had come from.

"It can be a lonely life out here, so far from everything." She turned to him and flashed a shy smile. "Listen to me. I don't mean to complain – forget I said anything."

He reached for her hand and wrapped it in his own. Laura stared down, and he snatched his hand away. She liked when he touched her, and reached down for his hand again, then she began to walk along the edge of the stream. "Sometimes you can see fish swimming in here. The boys used to love coming here to fish, and they'd even catch them sometimes. Not enough for a full meal, but enough to keep them happy." She smiled at the memory. "There's a spot a little further down where the fish are plentiful."

"You didn't tell them about it?"

She laughed then. "If I'd told them, they would have wanted to go every day. They would have fished the stream out, and there would be none there today." She glanced up at him. "I still haven't told them, but perhaps they found out for themselves."

They continued to walk until they reached the spot she spoke about. The fish here were still plentiful and thriving, and it warmed her heart. "I think I did the right thing. Do you?" Her heart pounded as she waited for his answer. She had no idea why.

"I'm certain you did. You did those boys proud. They grew into fine young men. That wouldn't have happened without you."

She smiled, but inside her heart was breaking. "It was a difficult time, not only because I'd taken on those boys, but my own situation…" She glanced up at him then, and the pity on his face sent her over the edge. Tears threatened, and she turned her face away, then hurried on, leaving him behind her.

Laura heard him hurrying to catch up, but she knew if she stayed, she would dissolve into a weeping mess. It might have been years ago, but her situation had been dire. When his wife died, Barnabas Adams rescued her and brought her to his home to look after those motherless boys. It was the best thing that could have come to pass.

"Laura…" He was right behind her now, and there was no way to avoid him. Chance pulled her into his arms, and she felt comforted. A stray tear rolled down her cheek, and she brushed it away. *Why did she have to go and spoil the day?*

"I'm sorry," she said quietly. "Not all memories are good."

"I know," he said gently, then brushed another tear away. In that moment, Laura knew she could happily stay like this forever. But she also knew she shouldn't.

"Do you want to talk about it?" She knew it was the last thing she wanted to do and shook her head. She hadn't felt so vulnerable for as long as she could remember since arriving at *Broken Arrow*. Not because of Chance, he made her feel safe. It was those memories she'd rather forget.

They stood there for several minutes, neither of them saying a word. Then she suddenly pushed herself back and away from him. She glanced up and he looked bewildered. "Are you sure you're all right? I don't mind…"

"I'm fine. A little embarrassed is all."

He frowned down at her now. "No need to be embarrassed. We're friends after all, and that's what friends are for."

Except lately she felt like Chance was more than a friend. She felt a trickle of something. Laura wasn't sure what it was, but it was there, nonetheless. And it was bothering her, because she couldn't shake the feeling, and she was certain Chance didn't feel the same about her. So if a friend was what he wanted, a friend was what he would get. At least for now.

Chance felt privileged that Laura felt comfortable enough to let her feelings out with him. He was more than a little grateful to have been there to soothe her when she needed it most. He'd always seen her as a strong woman who needed no one, but he had been proven wrong. After all, everyone needed a shoulder to cry on or an ear to listen to their troubles.

Problem was, he'd never really got to know her properly. In the past at least. Over the past months things had changed. It was a slow change, but he'd felt the shift. They'd gone from being mere acquaintances, to being something more. Laura had never given it a label, and he hadn't either, but it was there, niggling in the back of his mind. Now it was beginning to feel like there should be some sort of label. But Chance knew if he did that, he was likely to scare her away. It might even change the way he felt about her.

He inwardly shook himself. Why he was suddenly having all these crazy thoughts, Chance had no idea. They continued their stroll in silence, neither mentioning the incident again. He was certain Laura wanted to forget about it, and if that's what she wanted, that was exactly what she would get. He was a man of honor, and although he may not say much, he would defend her to the end.

He rolled his eyes. The last thing he wanted was to be melodramatic. It would go against the grain for Laura too, he was certain. He glanced down at their entwined arms and patted her hand. It was almost as though he wanted to reassure himself she was still there. She glanced up at him and smiled, moving a little closer.

What would it be liked to have a woman in his life? Not just someone to take walks with, but for all time. He'd thought about it so much lately and wasn't convinced writing away for a proxy bride would solve his problems. Or would even resolve his enduring wish for a wife. If he was honest with himself, he'd felt this way for quite some time. Years. The yearning had become far greater over the past months.

Laura had been visiting him at his cottage for some months now. Leaving him plates of food.

Sometimes just stopping by to say hello, then going off for a walk. He'd gone with her a couple of times, and it was pleasant, but he'd thought nothing more of it. *What if she was trying to tell him something?*

Was there a possibility the two of them could share something more than a passing friendship? His heart thudded. He was such a fool. And now Floyd seemed to be trying to push himself toward Laura, and that just wouldn't do.

Chance made up his mind to see where this friendship could lead them. And to somehow let Floyd know he was venturing into forbidden territory.

They finished their stroll with a comfortable silence. Laura seemed far more relaxed now, and Chance felt happy. He'd watched as she put her face up to the sun, letting its rays shine down on her. He tried not to stare as the wind whipped her hair up around her face despite the bonnet, and had forced himself not to reach out and push it back into place.

"We're almost home," she said quietly, turning to face him. "I've had a wonderful time today, Chance. Thank you – for everything." She smiled shyly, and warmth spread through him. *Did they have a chance at happiness together?* He wasn't sure how to proceed. Should they simply continue as they were, enjoying their strolls and chats? With Laura bringing him plates of food?

In theory it sounded good, but Chance knew emphatically that Floyd would hustle his way into her life if he was permitted to do so. It was no secret that Floyd also was contemplating marriage. Like Chance, he'd had no one in particular in mind, but now that he'd shown his hand today in his own subtle way, it was time for Chance to step up. He needed to let his intentions be known and ensure Floyd didn't push his way in before it was too late.

"It's been my pleasure," Chance said, swooping down to pick a wildflower, which he handed to her. "We should do it again sometime."

She studied him curiously. "And by some time you mean…"

Did that mean she was open to the idea? He certainly hoped so. Perhaps they should make arrangements today. Right now this moment. The last thing he wanted was to let Floyd jump the queue and ask to court Laura before Chance had the opportunity to make his intentions known.

"I could pick you up after supper tomorrow for a stroll?" He felt like kicking himself. Chance needed to be more assertive if he wanted to pursue the woman standing in front of him. "I mean, tomorrow after supper." There, that was better. Only it caused her to chuckle. It wasn't meant to be a joke.

She pulled her expression into one devoid of any emotion. "I'm sorry. I didn't mean to laugh, only it sounded kind of funny." She grinned then, and he knew she was right. "I'll be ready when you arrive." She opened the front door then, sniffing at the flower he'd picked for her, and made her way inside. She suddenly turned to face him. "Thanks for today, Chance. I appreciate it."

And just like that she was gone. His heart thudded. *Was there really any chance the two of them would get together?* He would have to wait and see, but Chance knew he'd have to make a concerted effort to win Laura over, to genuinely court her, otherwise she'd be snatched out from under him.

Chapter Four

Laura leaned up against the front door and sniffed the wildflower Chance picked for her. Sure, it was only a flower he'd stumbled across, but it was the thought that counted. Lately, she'd been feeling more and more connected to Chance.

She wasn't sure if that was because she'd been interacting with him more, or whether it was something else entirely. She did know she felt something. What that something happened to be, she had no idea yet. Hopefully it would show itself soon.

Floyd had taken an interest in her of late, but Floyd, as nice as he was, did nothing to warm her heart. He was a good man, handsome too, but he wasn't Chance.

"Did you have a nice walk?" Jacob studied her. She was still leaning against the front door, and he was probably wondering why.

"It was lovely," she said, holding out the flower for him to see. "We went down by the stream. I showed Chance where the fish are."

He grinned then. "You mean the spot you refrained from showing me and my brothers?"

"Yes, that's the one. You would have lived there if you knew."

She grinned at him, and he chuckled. "I'm sure that's true. You know," he said, stepping a little closer. "There is no reason you have to continue on here."

Her heart pounded and she gasped. *Was he asking her to leave?* "I…" She was suddenly speechless. *Where would she go?*

Jacob reached out and touched her shoulder. "I didn't mean…" He took a deep breath and started again. "Chance is obviously taken by you. I just meant, I don't want you to feel beholden to this place."

She nodded, sure he had more to add, and her heart beat slowed a little.

"Clarissa and I can cope. You deserve happiness, and the opportunity to live your life the way you want to live it."

"This has been my home for as long as I can remember."

"I know. And you are welcome to stay as long as you want. But you are also free to leave whenever you want as well."

She stared at him then. "There is nothing between Chance and myself."

He studied her again. "I've seen you together, and the way you look at each other. Give yourself a break and don't close yourself off to the possibility. That's all I'm saying."

She hadn't, and she wouldn't. Life with Chance would certainly be different to the life she had now, but Laura was not dismissing that prospect. In fact, it made her feel warm all over.

"Thank you, Jacob," she said quietly. "I'll give it some thought." She put the wildflower to her nose again, breathing in its fragrance. *Was it feasible? Could she and Chance get together, not just as friends, but as something far more?* The fact of the matter was, it was up to the handsome cowboy who had left her at the door.

If he asked to turn it into something more, Laura wasn't sure what she would say. After all, it would be life changing for them both. She would have to give it some thought, On the other hand, Chance may not even be thinking along those lines.

She shook herself inwardly. She was sounding like a schoolgirl with a crush on the older boy next door. Trouble was, she'd never had the opportunity to have a crush, plus Chance was the only man who had ever interested her.

Jacob left her alone, and Laura headed to the kitchen. She found a small vase and put that bedraggled flower in some water, giving it pride of place in the center of the kitchen table. It lifted her spirits just looking at it. *Was it because it reminded her of Chance, or was it simply because it was a flower?* She decided it was a little of both.

The fresh air had made her feel tired and she retired to bed. Laura lay there quietly, thinking about her future, and what that might entail. It was some time before she finally fell asleep.

Chance hitched his horse to a low growing branch. Not that he needed to – Samson would never run off. The Bay gelding had been allocated to him when Chance arrived at *Broken Arrow Ranch*, and they'd been together ever since. Like his rider, he was getting on, and Chance didn't know what he would do without him. He ran a gentle hand down the horse's back before joining the other two cowboys next to the small campfire they'd set.

Floyd poured him a mug of coffee and passed it over. "What gives with you and Laura?" The foreman had always been forthright and to the point.

He studied Chance as he waited for an answer, and Chance knew he needed to be careful with his words. "We see each other several times a week," he said, making it sound as though they were stepping out together when there was no such arrangement. They merely *saw* each other and mostly went for strolls around the ranch. Perhaps it was time to change that. To do more than take strolls together. The conversation got him to thinking. "We're going to dine in Halliwell later this week." It was an idea he had planted in his brain, and now regretted telling Floyd, especially since he hadn't asked Laura yet. The possibility was there that she would say no. His heart pounded. *What if she rejected his offer?* One of the reasons he'd never asked her out was the fear of rejection. But he was a full-grown man now, not little more than a teenager as he was when he first laid eyes on her. Besides, she was charged with bringing up those boys, and that wasn't a trivial thing for a teenage girl to have to do.

His mind went back to holding Laura in his arms. Despite the number of years that had passed, her dire situation back then still bothered her. Holding and comforting her, had haunted him ever since. And not in a bad way. He wanted to see her again, hold her again, but she may not allow him that luxury.

He was after all, a weather-worn cowboy, and she was a beautiful lady that any man would be proud to have on his arm.

"I guess what I'm asking is," Floyd took a deep breath and stared at Chance. "Are you two an item?"

Chance wanted to yell an emphatic yes but knew he couldn't. Laura had said no such thing, although there were signs that might be the case. Although it could be some time off. "We have been stepping out quite a bit lately, if that's what you're asking." It wasn't a lie, but Chance felt as though he'd embellished the truth somewhat. He needed to talk to Laura, but he sure didn't want to scare her off.

"I see." Floyd looked none too happy, but there wasn't a thing Chance could do about it. "I'm looking for a bride, and I thought since Laura was single, and available…" He paused then. "But that obviously isn't the case after all." He took a long sip of his coffee, then shoved his hat back on this head. "I guess I'll have to try and get a proxy bride after all."

Chance nodded. No way in hades was he going to tell Floyd he'd considered that option himself. The foreman might cotton on to the fact he'd been unsure about Laura. He still was to a degree – she hadn't exactly revealed her feelings to him. Nor had he disclosed his feelings to her. It was something he needed to do, and if Floyd's question was any indication, he shouldn't leave it too long or it might just be too late.

Chapter Five

Laura sat opposite him at the one and only diner in Halliwell.

This was a bad idea. An absolutely terrible idea. Chance was a cowboy, a rough and ready cowboy who didn't possess the same sort of manners a lady did. Heck, he'd have to keep himself in check the entire night.

He was already on edge.

Jacob had loaned him a buggy to bring Laura to town, and he fully appreciated it. After all, Laura didn't know how to ride, and anyway, what sort of man takes a lady to supper on horseback? He was revealing himself to be the unrefined creature he'd always believed he was.

"I've never been here before," Laura said, glancing around the diner. "It's quite lovely."

Well, that was a surprise. He was certain she would have dined there before. "I haven't been here before either. I guess it's a first for us both." He'd worn his best shirt, and put on clean pants. His work clothes certainly wouldn't do for a date with Laura. Apart from the stench of horse and cow, he wanted to give her the best impression he could.

He watched as she glanced around, realizing she was even more beautiful than he'd thought. The lighting in here was good, and he sat there taking in her beauty. "You look beautiful tonight, Laura." He could have kicked himself. Although he was genuine in his beliefs, it sounded disingenuous when he spoke the words.

"Why, thank you Chance. You scrub up pretty good yourself." She grinned at him, and a thrill went down his spine. It felt like a thousand nerve endings were dancing, and there was absolutely nothing he could do about it.

"I guess I do get pretty grubby when I'm working."

Her expression suddenly changed. "I didn't mean...you are always well presented. That wasn't meant as a criticism."

He hadn't meant to upset her. It was the last thing he wanted. This really wasn't going the way he'd anticipated. Maybe his expectations were far too high. "I didn't take it that way either." She smiled then, and his heart thudded.

Chance slid his hand across the table and covered hers. It felt good, better than he'd ever thought possible. She didn't pull it away, so he took that as a positive sign.

Next thing he knew, their waitress was handing them each a menu, and Chance pulled his hand away. He felt suddenly bereft, which seemed rather crazy. It wasn't as though he did it on a regular basis. The silly thing was, since that day down by the stream, he'd longed to put his arms around her again. *The question was, would Laura let him?* Last time was different – he was comforting her. If he did it again, it would be for a completely different reason.

He watched as she glanced over the menu. "Chicken pot pie does sound good," she said. "I'll try that, thank you."

Chance resisted the urge to screw up his nose. "I'll have the steak. Medium rare." He glanced across at Laura, who was staring at him as though she was waiting for something. "Er, thanks." She was smiling now.

He really did need to watch his manners. And he'd have to be careful not to curse. She would truly think badly of him if he let a curse word slip. It was different around the the other cowboys – they all did it from time to time. But ladies didn't like that sort of thing, and he was certain *this* lady would be most unhappy about it. Nope, he would not let that happen near Laura.

Their meals arrived, and he waited for Laura to begin eating before he did. Floyd gave him a few tips, which surprised Chance, particularly since Floyd had the same end game – to win Laura over. Perhaps he'd seen the error of his ways. Or at least the futility of pursuing her when he knew the two had a connection of sorts already.

Instead of eating, Laura reached for his hand and without warning, said the blessing. It was nice, and Chance appreciated it. How long had it been since he'd said grace out loud? Except for up at the big house that was. Honestly, he didn't know. It seemed rather redundant to say it openly when he was the only one eating.

She suddenly let go of his hand and began to eat in that dainty way he'd seen her eat before. *What else had Floyd told him?* Oh, right. *Keep your mouth closed while you eat.* He'd better do that too. The last thing Chance wanted was for her to think he was a pig.

Being out with a woman was hard work. There was far too much to remember. But Laura was worth it; he only wished he'd made a move toward her years ago. *Surely she was as lonely as he was?* Then again, perhaps not. Living in the big house, she was surrounded by people day and night. It was the nights that got to Chance. Living alone in that cottage was hard.

Not that he was complaining. Not many ranchers supplied their cowboys with their own dwellings. The majority had one bunkhouse for up to twenty cowboys, and that was it. Not on *Broken Arrow Ranch*. Every permanent cowboy was allocated a cottage. Each cottage had three bedrooms. That way, if they did decide to marry, there was room for a family.

Chance had worked on a ranch with a bunkhouse before he went to *Broken Arrow*. It was rundown and pretty grimy. There was an outside kitchen where they had to take turns to cook, and the grub was awful.

Now he had his own kitchen, and the food was still awful, but at least it was of his own doing.

"You're not eating?"

Laura's voice broke into his thoughts. Chance was a million miles away. "Sorry. Guess I was daydreaming. How's the grub? Er, food."

That made her chuckle. "It's really good. When you actually eat something, you can tell me about yours."

He knew she was poking fun at him, but Chance didn't mind. Just spending time with Laura made him happy. He wondered if she felt the same way.

He glanced down at his food and cut off a piece of steak. "Tender," he said without thinking. "It's really tender." He took a mouthful. "It's delicious." He went back to eating then.

They ate in silence, mostly because Chance didn't want to risk talking with his mouth full. Another tip from Floyd. Not that he did all these things. Oh no, he wasn't that uncouth. They were just things Floyd told him he should be aware of, so as not to ruin his night with Laura.

He suddenly felt on edge. *Was Floyd setting him up to fail by making him so aware of these things he would mess up?* Surely not – Floyd wasn't like that.

He mentally slapped himself. He was overreacting was all. He'd never gone out with a woman before, and it showed. Floyd was simply trying to help him. *Come to think of it, had Floyd taken a woman to supper before?* Chance thought not.

Once they'd finished eating, they were each given a dessert menu. Laura seemed hesitant, so he reassured her. "We can walk it off later if you want." She grinned at him then, which was a relief because the moment he'd said the words, he wondered if that sounded like he thought she was

47

overweight. Which was the farthest thing from the truth.

"I'd like that," she said quietly.

He would too. He always enjoyed their walks. They were often done in silence, but it was a comfortable silence, and he always appreciated their time together.

"It's nice not having to cook," she said, after the waitress left them alone. "Not that I'm complaining. I love cooking, but it's good to have a night off now and then."

He knew the feeling, but then again, he wasn't sure opening a can of beans and heating them up could exactly be called cooking.

Their desserts soon arrived, and Chance relished it. Except for when Laura brought apple pie or some other delicious treat for him, he never had them. Not unless you counted an apple or a slice of bread or two smothered in strawberry jelly.

"I have eaten far too much," Laura said as she took a sip of water. "I am looking forward to that walk though. I can't recall how long it's been since I came into town." She looked thoughtful then. "Barnabas Adams brought me here to replenish my wardrobe, so it has to be some years ago."

She closed her eyes momentarily, and Chance knew she was thinking about the former owner of the

Broken Arrow Ranch. He leaned across the table and squeezed her hand. "I miss him too," he said quietly, and she nodded gently.

"I don't know where I'd be now without him."

They sat quietly for a few minutes, then Chance pushed back his chair. Luckily he remembered to lift it and not let it scrape across the floor.

He then stood behind Laura and held her chair while she stood. Thanks to Floyd, he was the perfect escort for her tonight. At least he hoped he was.

They headed toward the door, and Chance paid for their meal on the way out. He helped Laura into her coat then shrugged into his, and they went outside. "There's not much to see here as far as I know," he said, but simply walking with Laura was enough for him. She hooked her arm through his, and they began to stroll along the boardwalk. The shops here were sparse, and if anything major was needed, the townsfolk went to the next town, which was a good hour away by buggy.

Laura turned to face him. "I'm not here for the view. It's the company that's important to me."

Her words made his heart thud. *Did that mean what he thought it meant?* His heart raced. He tried not to get ahead of himself, and worked at slowing his heart rate down. He took a few deep breaths, trying not to be obvious.

"Are you all right, Chance?" She guided him over to the wooden bench situated not far away on the boardwalk.

"I'm fine." he said softly as he turned to face her. He stared into her face and saw the genuine concern. "I promise." He also saw her plump red lips, and more than anything wanted to kiss them. *What would she do if he kissed her?* He resisted the urge because the last thing he wanted was to have his face slapped right now.

"I'm glad to hear it. Do you feel up to walking again?"

Instead of responding, he stood, taking her hand as he helped her to her feet. *She was such a petite thing – how did she think she would help the likes of him if he had collapsed or done some other such nonsense?* She didn't even reach his shoulders, and Chance was sure he could pick her up as easily as he would a feather.

But he knew better than to give it a try. Especially right here in the middle of town. Maybe one day out on the ranch, where there were fewer people around? He'd let it ride for a bit, but it was now on his list of things to do.

"Shall we," he asked, offering his arm again.

She accepted his offer, and they began their stroll again. He noticed her glancing about as they continued. It wasn't completely new to him. Chance did come into town now and then, but mostly for supplies from the mercantile.

Thinking about the mercantile gave him an idea. Although it was relatively late, they should still be open, so he'd see when they got that far.

Laura paused outside the shoe store, staring longingly at the ladies boots featured in the window. "They are pretty," Chance told her, but she shook her head.

"I don't need them. Perhaps one day when I have a need for new boots."

He glanced down. They were the same boots she always wore. *Would she accept them as a gift if he bought them for her?* He knew the answer before he'd fully absorbed the question. There was no way Laura would allow him to buy them for her.

It wasn't as though he couldn't afford them – most of the money he earned was sitting in his bank account, adding up week after week. His food bill was low, considering he mostly ate canned food, and he rarely bought new clothes. It wasn't like he went out often.

Her studied her, and it was like she could read his thoughts. "No. Absolutely not," she said firmly.

"I didn't…"

"Oh, but you thought it. I do not need new boots." She took off then, half dragging him further along the boardwalk, and it was all he could do not to chuckle, or even laugh out loud. Finally, they arrived outside the mercantile, and he sat her down on the wooden bench, and asked her to wait.

When he returned, Chance held a big bouquet of flowers in his hands. "These are for you," he said, handing them over.

"Oh Chance, they are beautiful," she said, as she leaned in to smell their fragrance. "Thank you." He could see tears dancing in her eyes, and wondered if this was the first time she'd ever been given flowers. It was highly likely, which made him feel particularly sad for her.

"Yes, they're beautiful – just like you," he said, then wondered if he'd overstepped. Instead of rebuking him, Laura stepped forward and rested her head against his chest. His arms came up around her, and it felt so right. She suddenly stepped back out of his arms, and he wanted nothing more than for her to lean into him again.

She stood there for what seemed like forever, looking up into his face. "You have no idea what these mean to me," she said quietly, barely above a whisper. Of their own volition, his hands came up and cupped her face, and he was an angel's breath away from her lips when he came to his senses.

"I'm sorry," he said, stepping back to stop himself from being tempted again. She stared at him momentarily, but didn't say a word. It made him wonder if she would have allowed his kiss or slapped him silly.

Either way, he couldn't risk scaring her away. After all, he was in this for the long haul. He wanted Laura Massey to become his wife, and not merely be his friend.

Chapter Six

Laura had thoroughly enjoyed her evening with Chance.

It wasn't just the meal, although that was nice. And it wasn't the flowers either, but they were beautiful. She knew exactly what was so good about it – it was the company she had kept.

Chance was such a caring man, and looked out for her all the time. Even on the ranch he made sure she was all right. He always walked her back to the main house, even in the daylight. It had become a ritual she really enjoyed. Not that she needed to be walked home – she was more than capable of getting herself back there, but she would never say no to his company.

She had no idea why Chance would say someone might accost her, because the ranch was so far out of town, no one would go there without good reason. It was an excuse, and they both knew it. Why he didn't just own up to that, she had no idea. Perhaps he felt a little too shy to say so? She quickly shook that thought away. Chance was a big burly cowboy, and he was far from shy – although if she thought about it, perhaps he was. They'd known each other for many years now, over a decade in fact. Until recently, he'd never made a move toward her.

It was a pity he hadn't because things could have been different. Laura had noticed him almost from the time she'd arrived. But she was far too busy with her young charges at the time, and had no opportunity, or even a wish, to get involved with a greenhorn cowboy. But he was far from that now. He was a grown man with far more appeal than he had a right to have. Only he didn't seem to know it.

Floyd on the other hand had made some advances over the years. He was a nice person, but he had been the boss's nephew. Well, he was Jacob's cousin, and that was even worse now that *he* was the boss. On the other hand, there was no spark between her and Floyd, and there was certainly that with Chance. Her heart fluttered just thinking about him, and it was far worse when he was near.

When he put his arms around her, it was as though she'd been enveloped by angels. She wished he'd do that more often.

"Did you enjoy yourself?" Laura shook herself out of her daze, turning to face Chance. He had one eye on the road, and the other on her.

"I really did," she said truthfully. "Thank you for inviting me." She brought the flowers up to her face and took in their fragrance, not for the first time that night. "And thank you again for these beautiful flowers."

"Better than a scruffy wildflower."

She glanced across at him. *Did he think the wildflower meant nothing to her?* If he did, he was wrong. That flower meant more to her than he could ever imagine. It might have been a spontaneous action pulling it out of the ground, but he went to that effort for her, and no one else. "I loved that flower. It meant a lot to me."

He gave her a sideways glance, and his expression told her he didn't believe a word of it. "I guess you'll put those flowers in a vase."

If he was trying to prove a point he was wrong. "Yes, I will, which is what I did with the wildflower."

Now he turned and stared at her. "You did?"

"I did. As I told you, it meant a lot to me."

He shook his head then, as though he still wasn't certain. Or was he trying to comprehend she'd done such a thing. "It's the thought that counts, Chance, not how much it cost. At least to me." She scooted closer to him on the seat of the buggy. "I'd forgotten how chilly it can get out here at night," she said. *It wasn't really that chilly, but the opportunity to get closer to him was there, so why not take it?*

He reached across and covered her gloved hands with one of his, keeping the other one on the reins. She wished she didn't have her gloves on, because she longed for his touch. She would take this for now, as it was the best she could wish for right now.

"The moon is big and bright tonight," Chance suddenly said. Did he think he had to keep up the conversation? Because he didn't – Laura was happy simply sitting there with him, being close to him, and just knowing he was there. She could imagine herself as Chance's wife. The two of them in the sitting room in front of a roaring fire. Laura with her knitting, and Chance – she wasn't sure what Chance would be doing. Maybe reading his Bible. All she knew was it was something she would happily do.

She could imagine them living a long and happy life together. They might even have a brood of children of their own, but she shook that thought away. They were both far too old to be thinking about children.

It was something they should have thought about years ago. This was the reason couples usually married young. And suddenly, Laura knew this was stupidity. Neither of them was thinking clearly. What was the point of marrying at their age? She wouldn't produce a child for Chance, and he would be unhappy at that turn of events.

Letting him pursue her was futile. It would end in heartache for them both.

Laura sat on the hillside at *Broken Arrow Ranch* and studied the moon. Chance had returned the buggy to the stable, and was now seeing to the horse. It gave her time to contemplate her earlier thoughts.

Chance was a good man, and the animals always came first for him. *She knew she would be missing an opportunity if she pushed him away, but wasn't that better than the heartache they would both experience if they continued this friendship?*

She'd always had a soft spot for Chance, ever since he'd been introduced to her when she arrived. He'd looked at her with those sad puppy-dog eyes, as though his heart was breaking for her. She wasn't sure it was all about her becoming nanny to three boisterous boys, or more about her own situation. If it wasn't for Barnabas Adams Senior, she would have been homeless and likely living on the streets.

It was something she preferred not to think about. Not then, and certainly not now. Her heart thudded at the mere thought of it. That time in her life had been relegated to the back of her mind, and Laura wanted to push it back there again. For some crazy reason, since she'd been seeing more of Chance, those unwanted memories forced their way to the forefront of her mind. Perhaps it was because he'd been so kind to her back then. She honestly didn't know.

"That's all done," he said, as he slipped down beside her. Laura gasped as she hadn't seen or heard him coming. "I didn't mean to scare you," he said, reaching for her hand.

His touch sent a shiver down her spine, and Laura wanted more. As much as she fought with herself about their relationship, she knew she needed Chance, but did he need her? Was he even interested in her other than as a friend?

She turned to face him and smiled. "The moon is brilliant tonight. It is even better from here." He studied her then, as though he knew she was trying to cover something up.

"We are blessed to live here," he said quietly. "Where else can you see this magnificent moon?" His hand came up to her cheek, and he moved slowly toward her. She studied his eyes, and his face, and couldn't help but move in toward him. She felt his breath as he was only an angel's wing away, and then she felt his lips on hers. The kiss lasted only moments, but it left her with the promise of more to come.

Laura felt as though she was walking on air after her night out with Chance. Or perhaps she should say, after that kiss. It was the first time she'd ever been kissed and was certain it showed. Chance would no doubt be far more experienced, being a cowboy and all. He might have lived on a ranch all his life, but that didn't mean he was innocent like Laura.

She'd been tucked away on the ranch at the main house all these years, and had not had the opportunity to step out with men. Oh, the ladies at her knitting circle had certainly tried to entice her. They even set her up one time, but she'd backed out. She had no idea who the man was, or even if he could be trusted.

But she knew she could trust Chance. Besides, Jacob wouldn't have anyone working for him who wasn't trustworthy, she was sure. Not that he interfered with his worker's lives, because he didn't, but she recalled an occasion where he took on an old cowboy a year or so back. Jacob had a distinct dislike for the fellow, as it turned out with good reason. It transpired he was part of a cattle rustling gang and had been casing the place.

She sighed. *What was Chance doing right now, she wondered?* Probably fixing fences, or rounding up cattle, or…she really had no idea what he did. Every day was different according to Jacob, but what would he know? He rarely set foot on the ranch itself, spending most of his time doing the record-keeping for the entire ranch, not just his own. And he was good at it.

She'd already spent far too much of her time daydreaming, and she needed to get something done. Laura cut the beef into cubes and rolled it in flour and spices, preparing it for a stew for supper. She made sure there was plenty so she could take some to Chance for his supper too. The pan was already heating up on the stove, and she'd added some bacon fat to help sear the meat. She'd collected carrots and potatoes from the garden and could begin to chop them once the meat was ready.

Later she would make cupcakes and something for dessert. She hadn't decided what that would be yet. Whatever it was, she knew Chance would enjoy it. And it wasn't like she was stealing from Jacob; he'd given her his approval months ago. He was a kind and generous man, and Laura enjoyed working for him.

Not that he'd asked, but if she married Chance, would she still be working for Jacob? Would he let her? Otherwise, she wondered what she would do with her days. Laura liked to be busy. Working at the main house was rarely busy, and went along at a steady pace. Now that baby Barnabas was a little older, Clarissa was able to manage better on her own, so that was one job she'd been relieved from doing.

She added the meat to the pan, then checked the time. She'd made fresh bread, and it must be just about ready. She opened the oven door and using a kitchen cloth, pulled one loaf out. It was nicely browned and looked perfect. It smelled delicious too. She hit the top of the bread with her knuckles and listened. It sounded perfect. Laura lifted the loaves out one by one, she'd made enough for at least two days, and placed them on a wooden board to cool.

"It smells delicious in here."

She'd know that voice anywhere. Laura spun around to face Chance. "What are you doing here?" There was no malice in her voice, only curiosity. It was rare for the cowboys to be this close to home during the day, especially at lunch time.

"I drew the short straw today. It's my turn to muck out the stalls."

That was good. At least she thought it was. Did it mean he would stink of...

"I took my boots off outside. Jacob let me in, and he didn't say I stink." He grinned then, and it made her smile.

"Then sit down. There is fresh bread, but it's still hot and needs to cool. I have thick vegetable soup on the stove, and it won't be long before it's ready."

"I couldn't possibly…"

He was going to argue about eating with her? He surely didn't mean it. We'll see about that. She pulled a mug out of the cupboard and poured him a strong black coffee. "At least have some coffee while you're here." Thankfully, he didn't refuse his favorite beverage.

Clarissa and Jacob soon joined them, and Laura placed a coffee in front of each of them. "You *are* joining us for lunch, Chance?" Jacob's voice was firm. It sounded more like a statement than a question.

"I…well, I don't want to intrude."

Jacob studied him then. "You're not intruding, you are family. If I know Laura, there's far more food than we'll ever eat. Consider yourself invited."

His eyes turned to Laura, and she smiled. He couldn't very well say no to Jacob. *Could he?* "Then thank you. I would love to."

Warmth spread through her. Chance was staying, and they'd have this extra time together. She was truly blessed.

Suddenly, Chance was on his feet. "What can I do to help?"

She put a hand to his shoulder. "Sit down and keep out of my way. That will be a great help." She grinned at him then, and he grinned back while sitting himself back down.

Laura poured four bowls of steaming vegetable soup, then sliced the still warm bread. The moment she sat, Jacob said the blessing, and then they began to eat.

"This is truly delicious," Chance said, filling his mouth with food again. "Thank you for inviting me." His eyes took in everyone at the table.

Laura suddenly felt as though a piece of her that was missing before had arrived. Warmth flooded her at the thought. Then suddenly she felt hollow. She knew Chance liked her, and he had kissed her, but did that mean anything more than a lonely cowboy pursuing the only single female on the ranch?

Women thought differently to men, and she really had no idea what was on his mind. It wasn't like Chance was a big talker, he rarely spoke. He was certainly hard to read at times.

Both Chance and Jacob finished eating at the same time, and Laura refilled their bowls without giving them a choice. "But I…" Chance began to protest.

"Just accept it," Jacob said. "Laura knows best." Chance shrugged his shoulders, and dug in. Laura knew from past experience he was a big eater, and she enjoyed making sure he ate properly.

He reached for a slice of bread and smothered it with butter. "You are the best cook," Chance told her, and she loved the compliment. One day she might be able to devote her days to cooking for this man, but she couldn't be sure if that was his plan. As things stood now, he was getting good food without any of the commitment.

He finished off his meal, then began to stand. "Thank you for a wonderful meal," he said as he pushed his chair back.

"Where are you going?" Laura asked, feeling a little hurt. "We haven't had dessert yet."

He stared at her. "You mean there's more?" Everyone laughed, and his cheeks turned red. She rarely saw him embarrassed, but it made him seem far more vulnerable. It was strange seeing the gentle giant that way.

"There's definitely more. You have your choice of Cherry Pie, Bread and Butter Pudding, or Blueberry

Muffins. Or you can have all three." She grinned at him then, and Chance seemed to brighten up.

She placed the desserts in the middle of the table, along with a bowl of clotted cream, fresh from the *Broken Arrow* ranch.

"It all sounds far too delicious, and if I didn't know better, I'd think you were trying to fatten me up," he said, rubbing his belly.

Laura had noticed over the past weeks that he looked far more healthy and attributed that to her cooking. At least now she knew he was eating well.

"Well, I really must go now," Chance said as he began to stand after finishing dessert. "Those stalls won't muck themselves out, and there's far more than that to be done." He turned to Laura. "Thank you for a delicious meal, and to you, Jacob and Clarissa, thanks for inviting me."

Jacob smiled, then stood. "You are always welcome, Chance. I hope you know that."

It made Laura feel warm all over at Jacob's words. And knowing Jacob, he meant every word of it. She walked with Chance to the front door. "I meant what I said," he told her, pulling her toward him, and enveloping her in a hug. "You are an amazing cook, and one day, some man will be lucky to have you as his wife." He leaned in and kissed her forehead, and then he was gone.

Laura stood frozen to the spot. *Did Chance mean he was not that man? Or was he dropping a backhanded hint that he was?* Either way she was more confused than ever. She thought they had something meaningful going on, but now it only left her wondering.

She watched as he headed toward the barn. *His mere presence made her feel good, but what if it was only one-sided, and he was just humoring her?* Laura was far more confused than she was before they had lunch together but wasn't sure what to do about it.

Chapter Seven

Chance stood at the doorway to the barn. Laura had looked confused by his words. *What was there to be confused about?* He'd just told her he wanted to marry her. Not in so many words, but that's what he meant. He thought she'd be happy, but instead she seemed…downtrodden, and very unhappy about the prospect.

Perhaps she didn't want to marry him after all. He sighed then picked up the rake to finish what he'd begun earlier. The sounds of horses neighing around him was comforting, but not as comforting as Laura's arms had been. Although he must admit she seemed to hold back. And that was after he'd uttered the words he thought she'd be pleased to hear.

It made him wonder if she'd gone cold on him. Chance's feelings had only increased. He was more in love with Laura now than he'd ever been, and not just because of her cooking. She was an amazing woman; he'd always known that, and wished he'd pursued her all those years ago. They would have been together for more than a decade already, instead of each of them enduring years of loneliness.

The repetition of mucking out the stalls was making him think stupid things. That's all he could put it down to, otherwise he had no idea where all these thoughts were coming from.

Of course Laura had feelings for him, otherwise she wouldn't continue to see him or to cook for him. She was a forthright woman who did not pretend about anything. Chance knew in his heart if Laura did not like him, she'd have sent him away by now. Told him not to continue seeing her. His instincts were right, he was sure of it.

He might tell himself that, but his heart was telling him a completely different story to his head.

He'd no sooner finished brushing down the last of the horses when Jacob called out. He was at the entrance to the barn, the closest Chance had ever seen him get to coming inside. Jacob was not a horse person, not since the incident, and rarely stepped foot on the ranch itself.

Chance made his way toward his boss. "I thought you might like to join us for supper," Jacob said.

Should he? So soon after making a fool of himself with Laura? "I'm not sure Laura would want me there." He pushed his hat back on his head, and scratched it. "She didn't seem too keen when she saw me out."

Jacob studied him. "Are we talking about the same Laura?" he asked as he chuckled. "*My* Laura is head over heels. I don't think it would take much for her to marry you if you asked."

Chance could only stare at him.

Jacob frowned then. "You are serious about her, aren't you? Don't play with her feelings because she's not as strong as you might think."

Of course he was serious, but he wasn't so sure about Laura. "Are you certain? She seemed a little off when I left her this afternoon."

"What exactly did you say to her," Jacob demanded, seeming a little testy this time. "She did appear upset when she returned to the kitchen."

"I said she'd make someone a good wife one day." When he repeated the words, he heard how bad they sounded, and realized how it must have come across to Laura. "I blew it, didn't I?" His heart thudded. *Had he killed his chances with the one woman he loved?*

"I hope not. You both deserve to be happy, and from what I've seen, the two of you are happiest when you're together." Jacob rubbed a hand across his chin. "I've heard there's a dance on in town this Saturday night. Maybe you could make it up to her by taking her to the dance."

He felt a little brighter. If he could prove to Laura how he felt for her, there might still be hope for the two of them. "I just might do that. If she'll let me, that is."

"You can start by getting cleaned up and coming to supper. You can ask her tonight and give her plenty of time to prepare."

"Women need lots of time to get ready," Chance said innocently.

Jacob chuckled. "There you go again, putting your foot in it." He laughed as he walked away. "See you tonight," he called back over his shoulder.

Chance had a habit of saying the wrong thing, and it worried him more than anything else.

Chance stood at the entrance to the dance hall, which was really the church hall, but it had been decorated up for the festivities.

It wasn't often they held a dance, but when they did, the town went all out. It wasn't even recognizable as the Halliwell Church Hall. There were streamers hanging from the roof, sawdust on the floor, and a band was at the back of the room, warming up for the evening's music. There were tables down each side of the room – one with drinks and the other with food. The ticket cost included refreshments, and he was looking forward to it. In reality, he was looking forward to holding Laura in his arms again, more than anything else the evening might bring. He hoped there was gentle music where he got to hold her close, not that barn dance nonsense that seemed to be all the rage nowadays.

His arm around her, he led Laura into the hall. They knew few of the locals due to the fact they both kept to themselves most of the time and rarely left the ranch. Albert and Elizabeth Dalton from the Mercantile were there and waved to them. Sheriff Dawson was also there, watching over the proceedings, along with the preacher. When he realized how few people he recognized, Chance knew he needed to get out more. Laura probably knew even less people than he did, which was rather sad for both of them. Not that it really bothered him that much. Chance preferred to keep to himself, and those he knew well. He didn't like to go outside of his own circle. He was a private man, and knew Laura to be the same way. It was one of the reasons they got on so well. At least he guessed that was the case.

The first dance began, and it was one of those boisterous songs he didn't like. The sort where you stomp your foot, and everyone changes partner. He planned to spend the evening with just one partner – the one he'd arrived with. Laura glanced up at him and screwed up her nose. "Shall we give this one a miss?"

He pulled her a little closer. "With pleasure. It's not my style either." Chance led her to a chair near the refreshments. "Would you like a drink while we wait for the real music?" He chuckled then, and didn't wait for an answer, instead heading to the table that held the drinks. At least he knew he might get a few dances if the band played some decent music.

Sitting next to her, Chance could feel her warmth, and a shiver went down his spine. *What would it be like having her as his wife? To wake up to her beautiful face every day? To love her for all eternity?* He could only imagine, but it was something he'd dreamed of for many years. Not once did he think it would ever come to fruition.

Romantic tones played in his ears, and Chance took her now empty cup, leading Laura onto the dance floor. He took her hand, and placed his other hand around her back. His only regret was she kept distance between them. Chance hoped to remove that distance by the end of the night. Of course, as a single woman, she had appearances to keep up. The last thing he wanted to do was ruin her reputation. Laura was an upstanding woman who deserved to be treated with respect.

The music stopped, and almost immediately, more began, this round also having romantic overtones. This time Laura rested her head on his chest, and she shuffled a little closer. It made his heart flutter. She glanced up at him and smiled, and warmth spread though him. What would she say if he asked her right now to marry him?

He opened his mouth to speak, then realized he didn't have a ring to offer her. He could have kicked himself. He was an idiot. You can't ask a woman to marry you unless you have the ring available. Halliwell was such a small town, and he wondered if the mercantile carried them. If the opportunity arose, he would ask Albert later tonight.

Right now, all he wanted was to stay this close to Laura. Simply knowing she was right there in his arms, made him feel privileged. Out of all the men she could have chosen, he was the one she picked. "This is wonderful," she said quietly. "Thank you for inviting me."

"Thank you for accepting."

Hardly another word was said between them for the entire evening. Instead, they danced and enjoyed each other's company.

The drive home was mostly in silence, although they did share a few words here and there. Laura snuggled up close to him as they shared a blanket to keep warm. The night got chilly, and there was even a little fog around, despite the warmth earlier in the day. "I had a wonderful time tonight," Laura said as she glanced up at him. She tightened her grip on his arms, and a thrill went down his spine. *Why did this woman's touch send his nerve endings into a frenzy?*

"I'm glad. I had a great time too." He glanced briefly at her, not wanting to inadvertently go off the road. "Because you were there with me." There, he'd said it. Told her she was the reason.

When he glanced at her again, she was smiling, and Laura squeezed his arm again. Chance wanted nothing more than to kiss her at that moment, and pulled on the reins for the horses to stop. When the buggy was finally pulled to the side of the road, he hooked the reins out of the way, and turned to her, cupping her face with his work-roughened hands. She stared into his eyes, and he leaned closer. "I'm falling in love with you, Laura," he said, right before he kissed her.

This kiss was not like the last where he merely brushed her lips. This was a real kiss, one that would tell her how he really felt. Her lips were soft and gentle, everything he expected them to be. She didn't pull away, and didn't deny him, but moved into the kiss and kissed him back. Chance didn't want it to end, but knew it had to before things got out of hand. He had far too much respect for Laura and refused to put her in a compromising situation.

They needed to move forward, and if he had his way, it would be sooner rather than later. He dropped his hands and moved back onto the seat. Her eyes pleaded with him, but Chance knew he was doing the right thing.

He pulled the blanket back over them and lifted the reins. They were soon on their way back to the ranch again.

Chapter Eight

The night had been incredible. She'd enjoyed every second she'd spent with Chance and had savored those moments. Then on the way home, when he'd stopped the buggy, she was dizzy with excitement. Her heart had pounded when he reached out to kiss her, and she'd enjoyed every second of it.

Then without so much as a word, he'd moved back into his seat, and lifted the reins. Soon they were on the way home again. She knew he had done the right thing. Chance would never compromise her reputation, not ever. Now they were on ranch property, and would soon be back at the main house. Home.

Would he kiss her goodnight, or would he merely dump her at the door and leave? She felt unsure since that kiss in the buggy. Whereas prior to that she'd felt confident things were moving in the right direction. Still, she could easily have taken more of his kisses.

Still trying to convince herself he'd done the right thing by her, Laura glanced at him as Chance pulled the horses to a stop near the gate to the house. Without waiting for him to help her, she stood, and Chance quickly climbed down from the buggy and came around to her side. "In a hurry to get away from me?" She knew he was joking as he quirked an eyebrow at the same time he grinned.

She was more than capable of getting down off the buggy without assistance, but she had no intention of telling him so. Laura liked the feel of his hands on her waist, and hoped that would lead to him holding her. *Why hadn't she told Chance how she felt about him, when he declared he was falling for her?* It was the perfect time, yet she'd let the opportunity pass her by.

His hands held her by the waist, and he lifted her gently from the buggy. He stared into her eyes, and studied them, seemingly lost in time. Slowly he put her feet to the ground, then pulled her close. "I miss you when we're not together," he said quietly, as though someone might overhear. There was no one about, so that was impossible.

"I miss you too," she whispered, unsure why either of them were being so quiet. Laura rested her head against his chest and listened to his steady heartbeat. He lifted a finger and brought it to her lips. She reached up and covered his hand, as though holding his hand in place, not wanting him to move it. "Thank you for taking me to the dance tonight," she said suddenly as she began to move away. "Perhaps I'll see you tomorrow?"

She felt suddenly hollow at the thought of leaving him, and she couldn't figure out why.

"Perhaps," he said, then pulled her close once again. His hand came up and brushed her cheek, then he leaned in and kissed her again. Laura sank against him, not sure she should be enjoying his touch, or his kiss. She only knew she felt differently when Chance was near.

When the kiss was over, she wanted more. She wanted him to hold her tight and never let go. The look on Chance's face matched the way she felt. They were both far too old to behave like lovesick teenagers, so it wasn't that. They simply enjoyed each other's company – that had to be the reason.

"Laura," he said, as she opened the front door. "I meant what I said earlier. I am falling in love with you."

He held firm to her hand, but it fell away as she slipped through the door. "I'm falling for you too," she said, then hurried inside.

She caught the look of shock on his face moments before she closed the door.

Chance led the horses into the barn. After unhitching the buggy, he brushed the horses down and fed them. Tonight had been the best night of his life. Holding Laura as they danced was far more than he ever anticipated. Thankfully there were plenty of slow dances, because truthfully, they were the only dances either of them was interested in. Barn dances might be fine for married couples, or even those who were just friends. But he and Laura had become more than that. She'd even admitted as much just minutes ago, and it had sent a lightening bolt through his entire body.

If he hadn't had to sort out the horses and buggy, he would have been dancing across the paddocks by now. He knew tonight had gone well, but he wasn't certain Laura had thought so. Now he knew for sure.

More than ever, he was confident enough to buy a ring for her. At least, he was pretty confident. Then again, what if she said no? The embarrassment would be far greater than anything he'd ever endured in his life. *Was it worth the risk?* His heart thudded – Chance had a lot of thinking to do. The only woman he'd ever cared for in his entire life was Laura Massey, and he was so close to having her for his wife. If he lost her now, it would be due to his own stupidity. He would kick himself if he let that happen. It would be like a knife to his heart, and he knew it would not be easy to carry on as if nothing had happened.

As he left the barn, he watched the windows go dark on the main house. They appeared the way his heart felt right now. Dark and without hope.

Chance woke up after a night of tossing and turning, and very little in the way of sleep. He was conflicted about the path ahead. *Should he forge forward with his plan to ask Laura to marry him, or should he just continue as they were now?* It felt as though they'd come to a point where a decision needed to be made, but the last thing he wanted was to frighten her away. But he also didn't want to discourage her either.

It was Sunday, and no decisions needed to be made right now, so he sat on the side of the bed and let himself wake up to the Lord's day with the joy and blessings that should be attributed to this day. He stood and stared down at the bed. One day, if he didn't blow it, Laura might share that bed with him. Share this house with him and share their lives. It had been a dream of his for many long years, yet he'd only recently had the courage to see it through.

They were having lunch in the main house again. He looked forward to spending the additional time with Laura. Of course he enjoyed time with the family too, but as always, Laura was his main focus.

He glanced around his cabin. It was nothing like the main house where Laura had spent the best part of her life. If he asked her to marry him, would she be content living here? His heart thudded. She was used to a far better lifestyle than he could ever provide. She was a lady through and through, and he was just a rough and ready cowboy. *Why on earth would someone like Laura want to marry the likes of him?*

Chance shook his head and ran his fingers across his unshaven chin. There wasn't a hope in hades she would agree to marry him. And he needed to get that through his head.

Chance collected Laura for a surprise walk. She had no idea, and wasn't prepared for it. "We won't be gone long," he explained. "It's such a nice day, I thought a stroll near the stream would be nice."

He knew it was one of Laura's favorite places to go, as she'd told him so last time they'd been there. "I'll be right back," she said, feeling quite excited about the unexpected visit. She grabbed a shawl and her bonnet, and they were soon on their way to the place that held so many good memories for her.

Laura hooked her arm through Chance's and closed the gap between them. "It's a beautiful day," Chance said, glancing upward. "Not even a cloud in the sky." He then glanced down at her and smiled. The smile then turned to a grin, and he covered his mouth with his hand. Curious.

"I thought you'd be working this morning." And she did. Normally Chance would be hard at work somewhere on the ranch.

He frowned momentarily, then smiled. "I started early so we could take this stroll together." He seemed rather pleased at his answer, which was even more curious. It left Laura wondering if he was up to something. What that could be, she had absolutely no idea.

They rounded the corner to the stream, and suddenly stood at the place she'd shown Chance recently – the spot where the fish congregated. "I love it here," she said quietly. "Watching the fish interact together, jumping in and out of the water. For some strange reason, I find it comforting."

He said nothing, but pulled her closer, slipping his arms around her back. "Laura…" She glanced up at him in anticipation, but he said no more. She sensed there was far more he wanted to say, but had to rein in his words. Instead he pulled her even closer, and enveloped her in his arms. Laura rested her head against his chest and listened to the steady beat of his heart. If she could stay like this forever, Laura would be the happiest woman in the world.

But it wasn't to be and couldn't be. They had their separate lives. She reveled in the fact she could see him several times a week, even if that was only for short intervals. Without warning, his fingers slipped in under her chin and he guided her face upwards. He stared into her eyes, and studied her, then his head came slowly down, and before she knew it, his lips covered hers. Laura didn't protest – she enjoyed his kisses, enjoyed every stolen moment she could get with Chance. They were two lost souls who had left it far too late to make a go of things. Chance was already in his forties; Laura wasn't far behind him. Why they didn't get together long ago, she'd never know.

But she did know – the three young Adams boys needed a governess. One who was focused on them, and not on running around having a good time. She had known it then, and on reflection all these years later, Laura knew she'd done the right thing. Even if her heart had been aching to get to know the handsome cowboy she'd caught glimpses of now and then.

It was all water under the bridge now, and finally she felt as though her heart was full to overflowing. She knew there could be far more, but Chance was a confirmed bachelor, and she'd be surprised if he ever married. In many ways they were like two peas in a pod.

His lips left hers, and Laura suddenly felt bereft. She reached her hands up and pulled him back down to her. It was a bold move, but she didn't want to lose this moment. He didn't complain, and his lips covered hers once more. Her hands slipped up his back, and Laura was certain he was the one person in the entire world who was meant for her. And she for him. It was enough to make her heart break, knowing they would never be as one.

They stood in silence for what seemed forever. His strong arms held her like there was no tomorrow, and Laura enjoyed every moment of it. "We should probably be getting back," he said quietly, then leaned in and kissed her forehead. His arms slipped down from around her, and it was as though a chill suddenly hit her.

"You're probably right. We've been gone for quite some time," Laura said reluctantly. She did enjoy her time with Chance, and never had any regrets.

They slowly made their way back to the main house – neither was in any hurry. It was such a beautiful day, and the company was everything she could wish for. Laura didn't care how long they took.

She opened the front door, and everything was quiet. Jacob would be in his study working, and Clarissa would be seeing to the baby. "Would you like coffee?" Before he could answer she found herself inviting him for lunch. Chance grinned at her as though she was missing something.

"That would be nice. Thank you."

They headed toward the dining room, and as they turned the corner, everyone began shouting *surprise!* "What the…?" Laura was confused and didn't say anything to begin with. Then she remembered it was her birthday. It was a day like any other, and she never bothered to even acknowledge it these days.

"Happy Birthday, Laura," Chance whispered next to her ear. She glanced up at him and smiled. This was his doing, she was certain of it. She wasn't sure whether to be happy he remembered, or annoyed that he'd caused such a scene because of her. Her heart told her happiness was far better. Especially when it came to Chance.

Laura sat dumbstruck at the activity going on around her and protested. "There must be something I can do," she said, attempting to leave the comfortable chair Chance had sat her in.

"Not a thing," Chance said as he grinned at her. "It's your birthday, we don't want you to do anything." He sat on the arm of her chair as she continued to watch the activity in the kitchen. It was difficult for

Laura – she was usually the one doing the bulk of the work.

She couldn't remember a time her birthday was celebrated with such gusto and knew Chance was behind it. In previous years the brothers, her former charges, held a small family gathering as a thank you for making their lives better.

She was so proud of those boys. Well, they were all men now, with families of their own. Tears threatened to force their way through, but Laura wouldn't let them. Today was meant to be a happy one.

She stared awestruck at the amount of food the three wives placed on the table, including Clarissa. Laura knew she'd done her job well teaching Clarissa to cook. She might not be the best cook in the world, but she could feed her family and know they were well looked after.

Laura thought back over all the years she'd spent right here in this house. All the happy times she'd had here. Chance squeezed her hand. "A penny for your thoughts." She glanced up and smiled at him.

"They are good thoughts," she said, leaving her hand right where it was. She felt happiest when she was with Chance. It had taken awhile, but Laura finally realized exactly where she wanted to be, and who she wanted to be with. Chance might not live in a big fancy house, but the important thing was who you spent time with, not the size of the house.

"Happy birthday, Aunty," little Mabel said, then grabbed Laura and hugged her. She might not be the child's real aunt, but Mabel was like family to Laura. All of the people here were the only family she'd ever had. At least from the time she'd come to *Broken Arrow*. Even the cowboys were family. Especially Chance who had become particularly special and important to her.

A tear slid down her face at the memories, and Chance wiped it away. "Why so sad?"

"Not sad," she said. "Happy tears." And they really were. These people were her people, and Laura knew they always would be. She brushed at her cheeks with the back of her hand, and Chance leaned in and kissed her forehead. He put an arm around her, pulling her close, and warmth flooded her.

"Everyone," Jacob said, glancing about. "We're all here, and the food is ready. Let's eat!"

Chance pulled Laura to her feet, guiding her to the table where he pulled out her chair and helped her to sit down. He then took the chair next to her. It was all very overwhelming. Her birthday wasn't that big a deal – she was another year older, but that was all there was to it. She glanced about the table. There seemed to be an underlying level of excitement that she couldn't fathom. Did they have something else planned she wasn't aware of? It bothered her until Laura realized they had probably made a birthday cake for her.

Mabel was overexcited at the celebrations. She was such a sweet girl, and so loving. Laura knew she had been blessed with this family. And with Chance. Jacob reached for Clarissa's hand, and everyone joined hands for the blessing. After that, Chance passed her the platter that contained roast beef and vegetables. The food looked and smelled delicious. More so for the fact she hadn't slaved for hours to make it.

Floyd and Karl were there too, sitting opposite Chance and her. Floyd seemed resigned to the fact she'd chosen Chance over him, and there were no bad feelings. It was quite a relief. Still, nothing had been vocalized with Chance – they had not been declared a couple, and she wasn't sure they ever would be. Although it would be nice to have him confirm their situation one way or the other, but Laura had no intention of asking him.

The banter around the table as they all shared the meal was heartwarming. It was something Laura had always loved about this family. Even when Barnabas was alive – family was all important. It was to her as well. Laura could not imagine her life without these people in it. They were her reason to live.

When everyone finished eating, she stood, about to clear the table. "Not today, Laura," Jacob said gently, and Chance reached for her hand, pulling her back down.

Mary, Abigail, and Clarissa all set about clearing the table, then Abigail carried in a birthday cake. It was as she suspected, and her heart fluttered at the trouble they had gone to for her. Little Mabel's eyes lit up at the sight of the cake. "Cake!" she shouted as it was placed on the table, and everyone laughed.

Everyone sang *happy birthday*, and Laura wanted to crawl under the table. Why she felt embarrassed she had no idea. Every person who sat around this table was celebrating her – she should feel pleased. And she was, but that didn't stop her from feeling a little uncomfortable about it.

"The biggest piece goes to the birthday girl," Abigail announced, passing it over to her.

There was no way she could eat such a large piece, and discreetly swapped it with Chance's when it was placed in front of him. He laughed at her antics, but said nothing. He knew she'd be mortified if he did.

After their meal was over, Chance led her back to the comfortable chair, where they had coffee. She'd been stressed when she'd discovered the family was holding a party for her but began to relax after a while. Now she felt completely relaxed, and even began to drift off to sleep for a short time.

"Laura," Chance said quietly. When she opened her eyes he was in front of her, down on one knee. She was fully awake now, startled by what he was doing. But it couldn't be true – she must have misconstrued the entire scenario. She glanced about. There was a hush that wasn't there moments ago. Chance pushed something toward her. *Goodness! Was that a ring box?*

Her heart fluttered and she felt lightheaded, despite being seated. Chance flipped the lid open on the box, and there sat the most beautiful engagement ring she'd ever seen. "I have loved you from afar for way too many years. Neither of us is getting any younger." He cleared his throat then. "Laura Massey, will you marry me?" He seemed to suddenly stiffen then, as he waited for her response.

At first Laura thought he might be joking. But the look on his face, and the ring box in his hand told her it wasn't so. A shiver went down her spine. *Wasn't this what she had prayed to happen, and not only recently, but for many a year?* She straightened her shoulders and shuffled forward on the chair. Laura licked her lips and stared into his face. The atmosphere in the room was palpable. Everyone was staring at the scene playing out before them.

"Say yes, Aunty," Mabel called out, suddenly breaking the silence.

"Yes!" Laura shouted, then threw her arms around Chance, knocking him backwards. She landed on top of him, and they both broke into laughter. "Yes," she whispered into his ear. "I love you, Chance Devlin. And always have." Tears rolled down her cheeks, and Laura knew she was the luckiest woman in the world.

The wedding was a quiet affair. They opted to hold it near the stream, in the place Laura loved so much.

Mary, Abigail, and Clarissa had fussed over her, and it had warmed her heart. Everyone treated her like one of the family and always had. Never in her wildest dreams had Laura envisioned herself as a blushing bride, but here she was – dressed in a beautiful gown, made especially for her. It was Jacob and Clarissa's wedding gift, and Laura couldn't be happier.

When she pulled up in the buggy, driven by Jacob, Preacher Joe stood waiting. Chance stood nearby looking nervous but very handsome in his Sunday best. Jacob helped her down from the buggy, and slowly walked her toward her groom. Her heart pounded. She'd waited for this day her entire life, and still couldn't believe it was happening.

But it was, and it was the happiest day of her life. When Jacob gave her away, a tear slid down Laura's cheek. Chance reached out and wiped it away. "You can't cry on your wedding day," he whispered. "It's bad luck."

"I'm marrying you," she whispered back. "That's definitely not bad luck." Chance squeezed her hand. Preacher Joe cleared his throat, and soon they were husband and wife.

Ten months later…

Chance sat on the edge of the bed and studied his new son. Colt had light brown wisps of hair, a button nose, and tiny little fingers. He looked more like his mother than his father, which surely had to be a good thing. Chance still couldn't believe he'd fathered a child, after all, he'd convinced himself it would never happen at his age.

Laura glanced up at him, the small boy swaddled in blankets and held firmly in her arms. "Your wife needs to rest," Doc Petersen told him. "She's had a long day."

"I'm fine, Doc," she said drowsily. Chance glanced at her and could see the doc was right. Laura looked totally done for, which wasn't surprising since she'd not long ago birthed their son.

He took the baby from her arms, and laid her back on the pillows. It wasn't long before her eyes fluttered closed. He leaned down and kissed her forehead, wiping a tear from his face as he began to quietly leave the room.

Doc Petersen followed him out. They were both confronted by the entire Adams clan.

"Well?" Abigail demanded. "Boy or girl?" She craned her neck trying to see the baby who would become her adopted nephew.

"It's a boy," Chance said, trying to rein in his emotions. "We've called him Colt." Abigail stared at him. "What? It's a strong cowboy name, and living here, he's sure to become a cowboy," he said.

Abigail held out her arms to take the baby. "He is beautiful," she said, holding back tears of her own. "You've both waited so long for this and deserve all the happiness in the world."

"My turn," Clarissa said, wanting to hold the baby.

"Don't forget me," Mary said as Clarissa cradled the baby.

It made Chance wonder if there might be a whole new round of babies on *Broken Arrow* in the next year or so.

"You did good," Jacob said, slapping Chance on the back. "The first of many perhaps?" He grinned, but Chance hoped he wasn't far from the truth. If Laura had her way, he was certain there would be more babies. Not that he was complaining. It felt good to be able to say he was a father. And *Broken Arrow Ranch* was the perfect place to bring up a child. He might not be rich, but this past year he was far happier and content than he'd ever been. Marrying Laura had completed him, and fulfilled his life. He'd always known they were meant for each other, but the timing was all wrong.

Now his life was perfect. He had a beautiful and caring wife, a new son, and a job he loved. *What more could he ask for?* Chance knew none of it would be possible without the love of his Savior. He had been a God-fearing man all his life, and for a while, Chance thought he'd been forgotten. Now he knew it was all about the timing and getting them together when they both needed it most.

He silently prayed his thanks for the blessings that had been sent his way.

The End

From the Author

Thank you so much for reading my book – I hope you enjoyed it.

About the

Author

Multi-published, award-winning and bestselling author Cheryl Wright, former secretary, debt collector, account manager, writing coach, and shopping tour hostess, loves reading.

She writes both historical and contemporary western romance, as well as romantic suspense.

She lives in Melbourne, Australia, and is married with two adult children and has six grandchildren. When she's not writing, she can be found in her craft room making greeting cards.

Links:

Website: *http://www.cheryl-wright.com/*

Blog: *http://romance-authors.com/*

Facebook Reader Group:
https://www.facebook.com/groups/cherylwrightauthor/

Join My Newsletter:

https://cheryl-wright.com/newsletter/